Clubhouse
Adventures

Disney's *Early Reader* books are designed for children at different levels of reading ability.

PRE-1 LEVEL

PRE-READERS

- Picture reading
- Repetition of words
- Short, simple sentences

1 LEVEL

BEGINNING TO READ

- Rhyming text
- Expanded vocabulary
- Longer sentences

2 LEVEL

INDEPENDENT READERS

- Phonetic words
- Opposites and soundalike words
- Greater sentence variety

3 LEVEL

READING LEADERS

- Wide vocabulary
- Challenging stories
- Chapter-book format

First Edition
Library of Congress Cataloging-in-Publication Data on file
ISBN 978-1-4231-1540-3

Manufactured in the USA
For more Disney Press fun, visit www.disneybooks.com

EARLY READER LEVEL PRE-1

Donald's Lost Lion

Donald's Lost Lion

A LEVEL PRE-1 EARLY READER
By Susan Ring
Illustrated by Loter, Inc.

New York
An Imprint of Disney Book Group

No, Goofy, no!
Surfing is not the way to go.

Goofy slides down a line.
Then he gets tangled in a vine.

No, Goofy, no!
Sliding is not the way to go.

Goofy sails next to a whale.
Then he flips onto its tail.

No, Goofy, no!
Sailing is not the way to go.

Goofy stops to have a treat.
Then he looks down at his feet.

Goofy wonders if you know,
A new way that he can go.

Yes, Goofy, yes!
Walking is the way that's best!

The Mystery of the Missing Muffins

The Mystery of the Missing Muffins

A LEVEL 1 EARLY READER

By Sheila Sweeny Higginson

Illustrated by Loter, Inc.

DISNEY PRESS

New York

An Imprint of Disney Book Group

Hello, everybody!
Do you want to come to my Clubhouse?
Well, all right. Let's go!
Just say, "Meeska, Mooska,
Mickey Mouse!"

Do you smell something baking?
It's my muffins!
I made them to share with my friends.
It's time for roll call!
Donald! Daisy! Goofy! Pluto! Minnie!

How many muffins are there?
Let's count them together:
1, 2, 3, 4, 5, 6.

Ouch! These muffins are too hot.

Oh, Toodles!
We need your help.
Let's see—a set of keys, a measuring tape,
a fan, and the Mystery Mouseketool.
Which one will cool the muffins?

Cheers! We've got ears!
A fan will do the job!
Now, just wait a minute while I turn it on.

Goofy, will you hold the muffins for me?
Thanks!

Ding-dong!
Did you hear that sound?
Let's go see who is at the door.

It's Donald!
He's been busy cleaning out his closet.
All of that work has made Donald terribly
hungry.
I bet he would like one of my tasty muffins.

Oh, no!
My muffins are missing!

Calling all clues!
We need to find my muffins right away!

Will you help me find my muffins?
Great! Donald wants to help, too.
He found the perfect detective hat.

Do you see anything we can use to find clues?
You're right! A magnifying glass will help us.

Calling all clues!
Do you see the handprint?
It means that whoever took the muffins
has hands.
Pluto, I guess you didn't take them.

Calling all clues!
Detective Donald has found a trail of crumbs.
It leads to a small door.

We need a tool to help us measure the suspects'
heights.
Should we use the set of keys, the measuring tape,
or the Mystery Mouseketool?

The measuring tape will do the job!
Goofy, you are too big to fit through the door.
You didn't take the muffins.

Calling all clues!
Donald sees a wooden box and a big
mud puddle at the end of the trail.
But where are my muffins?

Let's turn around and go back inside.
Yikes! The Clubhouse door is locked.
Which Mouseketool should we use to unlock
the door—the set of keys or the Mystery
Mouseketool?

Did you say the set of keys?
You're right!
Now find the key that matches the shape of
the lock. The triangle key will open the door!

Calling all clues!
Did you see the mud puddle outside the door?
Donald says that whoever took the muffins must
have stepped in the mud.

Donald checks Minnie.
There is no mud on her.
Donald checks Daisy.
There is mud on Daisy.
"You took the muffins!" he cries.
"The case is solved!"

Daisy cannot believe her ears.
She says she did not take the muffins.

Calling all clues!
Can you find something that is the same size
and shape as the muffin tray?

PUZZLES

MINNIE
DAISY
GOOFY
PLUTO

Good work!
The puzzle box is the same size and shape as
the muffin tray.
Daisy has an idea. She puts the box down on
the table. She turns the fan on.
What happens?

Calling all clues!
Look at where the puzzle box landed.
Daisy points to the mud-covered box.
"The muffins are in there," she says, "but the
lid is stuck because it's covered with mud."

Oh, Toodles!
Can you show us the Mystery Mouseketool?

PUZZLES

It's a crowbar!
Daisy uses the crowbar to open
the box.
Super cheers!
The muffins are inside, and now they are
cool enough to eat.
Come on, everybody!
It's muffin time!

Do you know the best thing about muffins?
When all your muffins are gone,
it's easy to make some more!

MICKEY'S BLUEBERRY MUFFINS

(From *Mickey's Gourmet Cookbook* © 1994 Hyperion, ISBN: 0-7868-8016-3)

YOU NEED:

3/4 cup of bread flour
3/4 cup of cake flour
1/2 cup of sugar
3/4 teaspoon of salt
2 tablespoons of dry milk powder

3 teaspoons of baking powder
1/4 cup of shortening
1/2 cup of water
2 egg whites
1/2 cup of blueberries, fresh or frozen

WHAT YOU DO:

1. Have a grown-up help you preheat the oven to 350°. Line the muffin tray cups with paper liners.
2. In a bowl, sift together flours, sugar, salt, dry milk powder, and baking powder.
3. Have a grown-up cut in shortening with a pastry cutter and blend until lumps are about the size of peas.
4. Combine water and egg whites with a fork; do not whip.
5. Add wet ingredients to dry ingredients and mix only long enough to moisten. Batter will be lumpy.
6. Spoon into paper-lined muffin cups and bake for 20 to 25 minutes, or until nicely browned.

Makes 12 muffins.

ARE WE THERE YET?

A LEVEL 1 EARLY READER

By Sheila Sweeny Higginson

Illustrated by the Disney Storybook Artists

Designed by Elizabeth Andaluz

DISNEY PRESS

New York

An Imprint of Disney Book Group

Let's go to the beach!

DRY
DESERT
10 miles

Mickey sees one cactus.

Minnie sees two lizards.

Are we there yet?
No. This is not the beach.

Donald sees three frogs.

Daisy sees four parrots.

Are we there yet?
No. This is not the beach.

SANDY BEACH 111 miles

ANTARCTICA 1000 miles

Goofy sees five seals.

Pluto sees six penguins.

Are we there yet?
No. This is not the beach.

Mickey sees seven deer.

Minnie sees eight rabbits.

Are we there yet?
No. This is not the beach.

Welcome
to the
CooL FOREST

Donald sees nine starfish.

Daisy sees ten crabs.

Are we there yet?
Yes!

This is the beach.
Let's have fun!

OVER THE RIVER

A LEVEL 1 EARLY READER

By Sheila Sweeny Higginson
Illustrated by the Disney Storybook Artists
Designed by Elizabeth Andaluz

DISNEP
PRESS
New York
An Imprint of Disney Book Group

Mickey got a letter.
Who sent it?

Dear  Mickey,

Come to our cottage for a picnic.

Use the map

from,

Goldilocks and the Three Bears

Mickey has to follow the map. Can you help?

First, to go out of the  Clubhouse,
find the round door.

To go over the _{river}, choose a tool.

Cheers! Mickey used the boat.

Next, go up a ⛰️ .
hill

Find the highest one.

Hot dog! We found it!
Now, to go through the dark forest,
choose a tool.

dark forest

Cheers! Mickey used the fireflies. To go across the pond , count the stones.

Good job! There were five stones. Now, to go down the 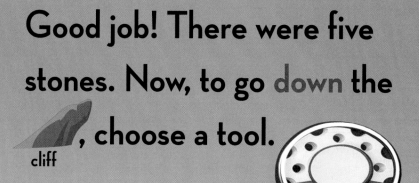, choose a tool.

cliff

Cheers! Mickey used the rope. Next, go between the 🌲🌲. Find the tallest ones.

trees

Hot dog! We're almost there! To go under the ,

rocks

choose a tool.

Super cheers! Mickey used
the shovel. Now, go into the
🏞️ . Find the green one.

meadow

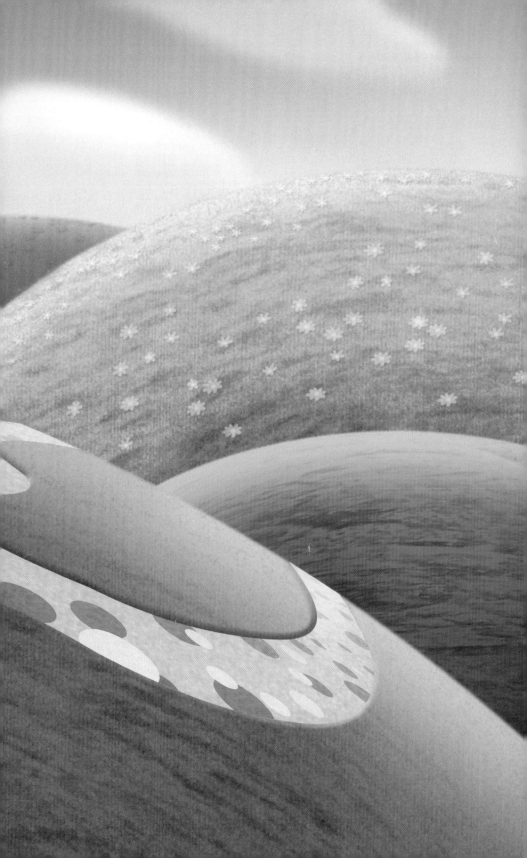

Hot dog! We're here!
It's time to eat!

Pluto's Best

A LEVEL PRE-1 EARLY READER

By Susan Ring

Illustrated by Loter, Inc.

DISNEY PRESS

New York

An Imprint of Disney Book Group

Meeska, Mooska, Mickey Mouse!

Let's go into my Clubhouse.

is going to be in a contest.

Pluto

 is going to be in it, too.

Butch

They both want to win the big .

prize

Oh, Toodles!

Here are today's Mousketools:

five yellow  , a , and a .

balls   life preserver   whistle

Goofy begins the contest.

Oh, no!  only has one ●.
Pluto   ball

He needs to juggle six ●●●●●●.
                        balls

Oh, Toodles!

Do you see a tool that could help Pluto?

Yes! Pluto can use the five yellow ●●●●●.
     Pluto   balls

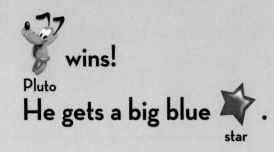 wins!

Pluto

He gets a big blue ★ .

star

 and  run and jump.

Pluto Butch

Oh, no! Pluto, come back!

 can't hear us.

Pluto

Oh, Toodles!

Which tool can we use to call  ?

Pluto

Cheers! We'll use the

 .

whistle

 **Butch** **wins!**

He gets a big red ⭐ .
star

Butch wins the next game—wagon pulling.

He has two ★★ **stars**.

How many does 🐶 have?

Pluto

Now it is time to swim.

Who will get to the end of the pool first?

Oh, no! Butch needs help.

Oh, Toodles!

Will the life preserver help save Butch?

Yes!

Go, , go!
Pluto
You can help .
Butch
 helps  get to the end!
Pluto Butch

Butch wins!

He gets a big red ★ star .

He gives it to 🐕 .
Pluto

Now  and have the same number

Butch   Pluto

of ⭐⭐ .

stars

Let's count them!

Yes, they have two ⭐⭐ each.

stars

They both share the big 🏆 !

prize

Disney

MICKEY MOUSE
CLUBHOUSE

Mickey's Campout

Mickey's Campout

A LEVEL PRE-1 EARLY READER

By Susan Ring

Illustrated by Loter, Inc.

DISNEY
PRESS

New York

An Imprint of Disney Book Group

Hi, everybody!

Can you say Meeska, Mooska,

Mickey Mouse?

Let's go to the  !
Clubhouse

We are going camping.

First we will set up a tent.

Then we will have a  .
campfire

Toodles has our Mouseketools.

They are a  , a  , and a  .
pot   woodpecker   Mystery
                                  Mousetool

We are all here!

Minnie , Daisy , Donald , Pluto , Goofy ,

and Pete are going camping, too.

Is everybody ready?

Don't forget the tents.

Camping is fun!

Let's set up the first  .

This tent is for Mickey and Donald.

tent

Mickey   Donald

Uh-oh. The tent is not right.

The ⟋ is too long.

pole

How can we make it shorter?

Mickey can't fix the  .
tent

Donald can't fix the tent.

Can anyone fix the tent?

We must cut the ⟋ .
pole

Oh, 🔵 !
Toodles

Which tool should we use?

That's right!

The  ! He can cut the _____ .

woodpecker   pole

Now, Donald and Mickey can set up

their _____ .

tent

and tried to set up their tent.

Daisy   Minnie

The tent should look like a big .

balloon

But it is flat like a .

plate

Daisy can't fix the tent.

Minnie can't fix the tent.

Who can fix the tent?

The tent should look like a big 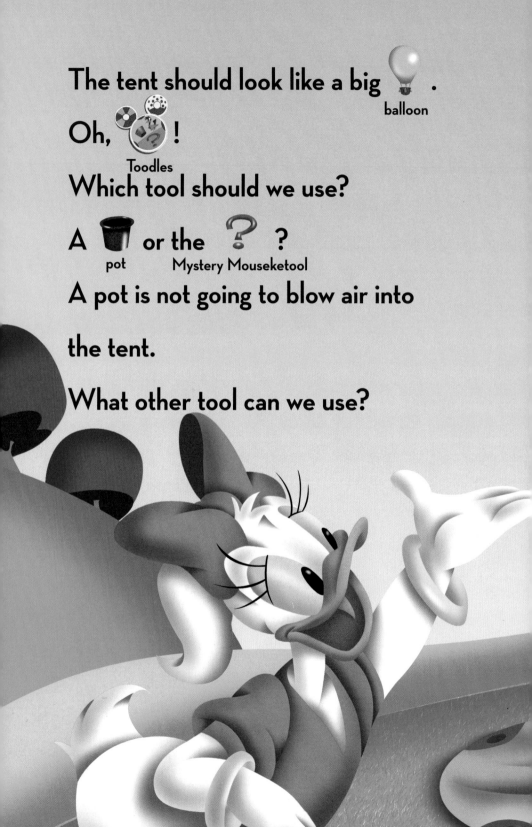 .

balloon

Oh, ! !

Toodles

Which tool should we use?

A or the ?

pot   **Mystery Mouseketool**

A pot is not going to blow air into

the tent.

What other tool can we use?

That's right! The  is a fan.
Mystery Mouseketool

It will blow air into the tent.

It will make the tent look like a big balloon.

Now, Daisy and Minnie can set up their tent.

and were going to set up

Pete Goofy

their , but is sleeping on

tent Pete

top of it!

What can do?

Goofy

Which tool should we use?

Oh, !

Toodles

Will the pot do the trick?

Yes! The  **pot** is the right tool for  **Goofy** !

 **Pete** wakes up!

Now  **Goofy** and  **Pete** can set up their

 **tent** .

All of the 🏕️ are up.
tents

Mickey and Donald make a 🔥.
campfire

Minnie has a special treat.

It is one of the best things about

camping: 🍡 !
marshmallows